A Tiger Tale

by Ann Whitehead Nagda
Illustrated by Paul Kratter

For my husband, Jagdish — A.W.N.

To my loving family, Joel, Marshall and Tia. This book is also dedicated to preserving the natural habitat of the magnificent tiger — P.K.

Published by Soundprints Division of Trudy Corporation, Norwalk, Connecticut.

Book design: Marcin D. Pilchowski
Editor: Laura Gates Galvin
Editorial assistance: Chelsea Shriver

First Edition 2003
10 9 8 7 6 5 4 3 2
Printed in China

Acknowledgments:
  Our thanks to Fiona Sunquist, Bengal tiger specialist, for her curatorial review.
  The author would like to thank Bhim Gerung and Dave Smith for their invaluable help in researching tigers at Chitwan National Park.

Library of Congress Cataloging-in-Publication Data is on file with the publisher and the Library of Congress.

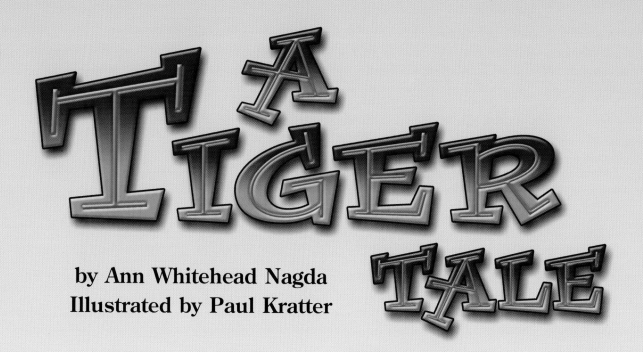

A TIGER TALE

by Ann Whitehead Nagda
Illustrated by Paul Kratter

Soundprints
Where Children Discover...

4

Thick fog covers the Chitwan Valley in southern Nepal where a Bengal tigress hunts. Hidden in the tall grass, she watches a herd of deer grazing by the river. The deer would make a good meal for Tigress.

Tigress quietly moves closer to them. Just as she is ready to pounce, one of the deer catches her scent and cries out. The herd runs away.

Tigress stands up and stretches. She will hunt again later. She walks to a bushy spot in the forest and softly calls *ahh-oooo, ahh-oooo.* Three tiger cubs rush from a bamboo thicket. They greet their mother with excited squeaks. They run around her in circles. They are very hungry.

Tigress nuzzles her cubs, then lays on her side to let them nurse.

Tigress leads her cubs through the forest.
She steers her cubs away from a nearby bear.
He could be dangerous!

The male cub climbs up a tree. Another
cub starts to follow her brother into the tree,
but he playfully pushes her down!

Soon Tigress and her cubs come to a lake. A huge rhino stands in the water. Two birds land on the rhino's back! Near the edge of the lake, three young pigs root in the mud. They would make a tasty meal for the tigers. Tigress crouches low and moves toward them.

Tigress creeps closer and closer. Suddenly, the tiger cubs chase a peacock out of the tall grass. The piglets are startled and start to squeal loudly.

A mother pig charges out of the grass, grunting furiously. She stands guard by her piglets. Tigress decides not to fight with the angry pig and calls for her cubs to follow her.

Tigress leads her cubs toward the river. Near the bank is a grove of cotton trees with bright red flowers. Monkeys sit high in the tree branches. They stick their faces into the flowers to drink the sweet nectar. Deer crowd beneath the tree to eat the blossoms that have fallen to the ground. When Tigress sees the deer, she crouches low in the grass.

The deer do not see Tigress. One of the deer moves toward her to reach a flower. Tigress leaps from her hiding place and grabs the deer! The other deer flee.

As Tigress and her cubs start to eat, a male tiger approaches. He is a stranger passing through their territory. Tigress knows that he might hurt her cubs. She quickly leads them away. To save her cubs, Tigress must let the stranger have the deer.

Tigress takes her cubs to a stream where they will be safe. She sits in the water to cool herself. She swishes her tail and showers her back with water. When she comes out of the water, the cubs lie down beside her and whine. They are hungry. Tigress nuzzles and licks her cubs to comfort them.

Later, when the cubs fall asleep, Tigress leaves them to go hunting.

Tigress heads back to the spot where she left the deer. She hears tigers fighting! One of them is her mate—the father of the cubs—and the other is the male who stole the deer from her. With a roar, her mate rises on his hind legs. He bats at the intruder with his paws.

Tigress hurries away. She must find food for herself and her cubs! All night long she hunts alone, but she does not catch anything.

In the early morning, Tigress returns to her cubs. They are happy to see her. As Tigress leads the cubs through the forest, the cubs chase and tumble over each other, racing far ahead. All at once, a large male deer calls out in alarm.

The cubs' play has startled the deer out of hiding. He bounds toward Tigress. Tigress leaps up and grasps the deer by its throat. The deer shakes her off.

Tigress doesn't give up! She races after the injured deer and grabs it again. The deer falls at the edge of a lake. Tigress carries the deer away from the water, and the hungry crocodiles that live there. The cubs leap and jump in excitement. As they settle down to feast, a large male tiger comes toward them out of the forest.

It's the cubs' father! He patiently waits to eat until Tigress and the cubs have had their fill.

With full stomachs, Tigress and her family all rest, their hunger satisfied at last.

THE BENGAL TIGER LIVES IN SOUTHEAST ASIA

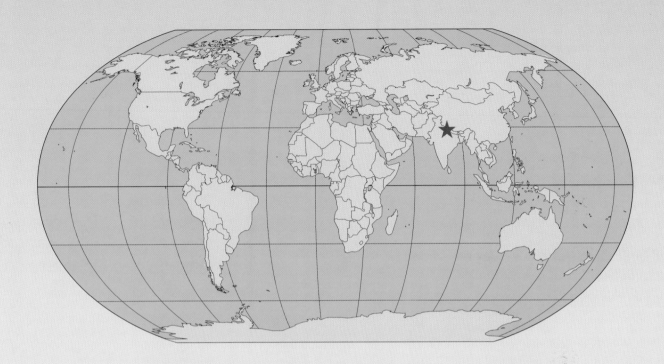

ABOUT THE BENGAL TIGER

Bengal tigers live in tropical jungles, brush, marshlands and tall grassland areas of Bangladesh, Nepal, India, Bhton and Burma.

Tigers can weigh up to 500 pounds and grow up to 10 feet long, making them the largest existing members of the cat family. The roar of the Bengal tiger can be heard over two miles away! They are the only big cats that enjoy lounging in water.

Tigers eat large animals such as deer, antelope and buffalo and smaller animals such as monkeys. They can eat as much as 80 pounds of food at one time.

Tigers hunt mostly at dusk and dawn and their stripes help them hide in the shadows of tall grasses. Not only is their fur striped, but their skin is striped, too!

Tigers can live up to fifteen years in the wild, or eighteen years in captivity.

▲ Sloth bear

▲ Chital deer

▲ Langur monkey

▲ White-backed vultures

▲ Sal tree

▲ Green parakeet

▲ Wild boar sow and piglets

▲ Bengal tiger

▲ Elephant grass

▲ Rhesus macaque

▲ Greater one-horned rhinoceros

▲ Mynah bird

▲ Sambar

PICTORIAL GLOSSARY

▲ Bar-headed geese

▲ Lapwing

▲ Peacock

▲ Common kingfisher

▲ Marsh mugger crocodile